JIG, FIG, AND MRS. PIG

PETER HANSARD

illustrated by FRANCESCA MARTIN

CANDLEWICK PRESS
CAMBRIDGE, MASSACHUSETTS

n a big old house on the far side of the bridge lived Mrs. Pig, her son Fig, and their servant Jig. If Mrs. Pig was sour and cross all day, it was simply because that was her way. Mrs. Pig was mingy, stingy, and mean. And Fig, like his mother, was spoiled, bad-tempered, and an awful pain.

Of course, Mrs. Pig loved her son Fig because he was so much like herself.

"He's the apple of my eye," Mrs. Pig would say fondly. "He's my Figsy-pigsy darling."

But if little Jig was cold, tired, hungry, or bullied by nasty Fig, Mrs. Pig hardly even noticed.

One of Jig's most difficult tasks was fetching the milk. Every single morning, rain or shine, Jig had to carry two heavy wooden pails all the way to town and back again.

All the same, despite day after day of endless drudgery, Jig would take up the pails and, in her sweet, clear voice, sing merry little songs so that she might forget that her load was heavy and the way was long.

One day, when returning home with the milk, Jig met an old pig.

"Please, may I take a sip from your pail?" asked the old pig. "I am very poor and very tired."

"Oh, of course you may," said Jig, even though she knew that Mrs. Pig would be very angry and give her no lunch. "Please have as much as you want."

"You are ever so kind," said the old pig. "You shall have your reward."

With a sudden flash and a sudden crash and in a shimmer of golden light, the poor old pig changed into a wizard.

The wizard waved his magic wand once, waved his wand twice, and waved his wand thrice.

"Higgledy-piggledy, jiggery-spoke! I shall give you this gift: Along with every word you speak, there will fall from your mouth a nugget of gold or a precious diamond."

Then with another flash and another crash, the wizard was gone.

When Jig got home, she found herself in big trouble.

"Some of my milk is missing!" shouted Mrs. Pig. "You careless, stupid thing. There will be no lunch for you today and no dinner either."

"Quite right," said Fig, sticking out his tongue. "Imagine spilling our milk. What a silly piggy she is!"

"I'm ever so sorry," said Jig, as two gleaming nuggets and two brilliant diamonds popped out of her mouth.

Mrs. Pig snatched them up at once. "Where did you get these?" she demanded angrily.

Mrs. Pig and Fig looked at Jig in astonishment as Jig told them all about the wizard. When she had finished, a glittering heap of gold and diamonds lay on the kitchen floor.

The next day, Mrs. Pig told Fig to go to town for the milk instead of Jig.

"Surely you don't expect me to carry those heavy pails?" Fig moaned.

"I most certainly do!" said Mrs. Pig firmly. "Go at once, and keep an eye out for that old pig. I want gold! I want diamonds! And I want them now!"

Moaning and groaning, Fig took up the pails and set off for town.

On the way home, Fig met a rich
young pig.

"I say," said the rich young pig,
"will you spare me a drop to drink?"

"No, I won't!" snapped nasty Fig.
"I haven't lugged this rotten milk all
the way from town just to waste it on
the likes of you. Go away!"

"You are not at all nice," said
the rich young pig. "You shall have
your reward."

With a sudden flash and a sudden crash and a shimmer of golden light, the rich young pig changed into a wizard.

The wizard waved his wand once, waved his wand twice, and waved his wand thrice.

"Higgledy-piggledy, figgery-joke! I shall give you this gift: Along with every word you speak, there shall fall from your mouth a warty toad or a slithery snake."

Then with another flash and another crash, the wizard was gone.

"Speak to me!" said Mrs. Pig, when Fig arrived home. "Speak to me, my Figsy-pigsy darling."

"I don't have any gold or diamonds," cried Fig, spraying his mother with toads and snakes. "But it's not my fault! If Jig hadn't given our milk to that old pig in the first place, this would not have happened!"

Mrs. Pig screamed in horror. "I hate toads and I can't stand snakes! Get away from me, you horrible, nasty, nasty thing!"

Pushing Fig aside, Mrs. Pig ran squealing from the house. But no matter how fast she ran, nasty Fig stayed right behind her, clinging desperately to her apron strings.

Jig stood and watched as Mrs. Pig and Fig, in a great clamor of squeals, shrieks, screams, and grunts, raced away into the distance.

Then, after they had quite disappeared from view, she turned and went back inside.

"Oh, it's lovely having the house to myself," said little Jig. She put eight jewels in her pocket and sang this song:

The sight of gold and diamonds
Gives everyone a thrill;
Yet kindly words and actions
Can be more precious still.

And so, as time went by, Jig became happier and richer. Of course, she did sometimes wonder if Mrs. Pig and nasty Fig would ever come back, but as it happens . . . they never, never did.

For Astrid

P.H.

———————

For Derek

F.M.

Text copyright © 1995 by Peter Hansard
Illustrations copyright © 1995 by Francesca Martin

First U.S. edition 1995

Library of Congress Cataloging-in-Publication Data
Hansard, Peter.
Jig, Fig, and Mrs. Pig / by Peter Hansard ; illustrated by Francesca Martin.—1st U.S. ed.
Summary: In this variation on the Perrault fairy tale "The Fairies," magic chastises
a rude young pig and rewards his hardworking female servant.
ISBN 1-56402-540-3
[1. Fairy tales. 2. Folklore—France.] I. Martin, Francesca, ill. II. Title.
PZ7.H19822Ji   1995
398.2—dc20 [E]   94-10435

2 4 6 8 10 9 7 5 3 1

Printed in Italy

The pictures in this book were done in watercolor.

Candlewick Press
2067 Massachusetts Avenue
Cambridge, Massachusetts 02140

Carbon-Oxygen and Nitrogen Cycles

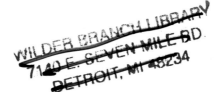

Rebecca Harman

Heinemann Library
Chicago, Illinois

...Melanie Copland
Design: Victoria Bevan and AMR Design
Illustration: Art Construction and
David Woodroffe
Picture Research: Mica Brancic and
Helen Reilly
Production: Duncan Gilbert

Originated by Chroma Graphics (Overseas) Pte. Ltd
Printed in China by WKT Company Limited

09 08 07 06
10 9 8 7 6 5 4 3 2

Library of Congress Cataloging-in-Publication Data
Harman, Rebecca.
  Carbon-oxygen and nitrogen cycles / Rebecca Harman.
    p. cm. -- (Earth's processes)
  Includes bibliographical references and index.
  ISBN 1-4034-7060-X (lib. bdg.) -- ISBN 1-4034-7067-7 (pbk.)
  1. Atmospheric chemistry--Juvenile literature. 2. Atmospheric carbon dioxide--Juvenile literature.
3. Oxygen--Juvenile literature. 4. Atmospheric nitrogen compounds--Juvenile literature. I. Title. II.
Series.
  QC879.6.H37 2005
  551.51'1--dc22

                                                          2005010643

Acknowledgments
The Publishers would like to thank the following for permission to reproduce photographs:
Alamy Images/Jason Friend **p.9**; Alamy Images/Agripictures **p.6**; Alamy Images/Ron Scott **p.16**;
Alamy Images/Oote Boe **p.19**; Alamy Images/Ashley Cooper **p.25**; Corbis **pp.20, 26**; Corbis/Gary
Braasch **p.8**; Corbis/Tim Davies **p.13**; Corbis/Larry Lee Photography **p.21**; Digital Vision **pp.4, 12**;
Getty Images/PhotoDisc **pp.17, 18, 22, 29**; Science Photo Library **p. 27**; Still Pictures/SJ Krasemann
p.10.

Cover photograph of tree stump in British Columbia, Canada reproduced with permission of
Corbis/Gunter Marx.

The Publishers would like to thank Nick Lapthorn for his assistance in the preparation of this book.

Every effort has been made to contact copyright holders of any material reproduced in this
book. Any omissions will be rectified in subsequent printings if notice is given to the Publishers.